CHARLIE
AT THE
ZOO

Marcus Pfister

Translated by J. Alison James

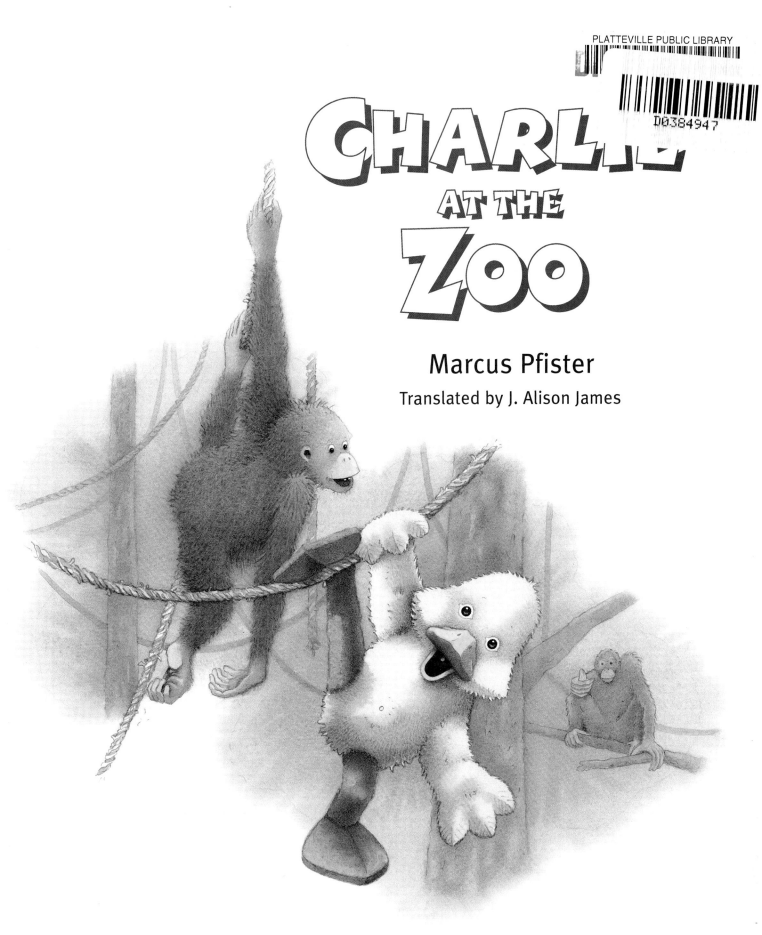

NORTHSOUTH
BOOKS

NEW YORK / LONDON

Who is that peeking out from the reeds?

It's Charlie, the oldest of five ducklings, who lives with his family in a little pond. Every time Charlie sees something he doesn't understand, he just has to find out what it is.

"What's that?" he asks his mother.

And if mother doesn't know, Charlie goes off to find out for himself. Charlie's mother has her wings full with four other ducklings, and is used to having her oldest swim off for the day. But he *must* be back home in time for dinner.

One day Charlie was out exploring as usual, when he heard a strange sound coming from the reeds. What was that? Were there other ducks around here?

Charlie went to find out.

It wasn't a duck, but an odd green animal. It sat on a leaf, blew up both cheeks, and said "*croak!*" It looked funny, and sounded funny too!

Charlie opened his beak to ask, "What are you?" But before he could speak, whatever it was took a huge leap and plunged into the water.

What a shame!

Now two long thin legs waded into view.
They belonged to a giant bird that stalked
through the reeds and poked his pointed beak
again and again into the water. He poked right
where the funny green animal had disappeared.

Charlie hid behind some reeds and did not
make a peep.

Charlie was starting to feel a little bit uncomfortable among the reeds. Who knew what else was in the water?

So he climbed up on the shore and looked around for his family. He couldn't see them. He'd have to go across the meadow to find them. But first, he wanted to take a little nap, so he lay down in the grass.

Charlie was almost asleep
when a giant shadow fell across
him, and something moist and
rough grazed his face.

"Oh!" cried Charlie. "What's that?"

"*Moooo!*" said the brown monster with the giant tongue, shaking her head. "Yuck," she said. "First I nearly ate that zoo hat, and now I licked a duck!"

Charlie shook his head. "What's a zoo hat?"

"It's a hat from the zoo."

"What's a zoo?"

"A zoo is a place where animals from all over the world live. You can see them and learn all about them."

"And where is this zoo?" Charlie wanted to know.

"Right there, across my pasture."

"This I have to see!" Charlie cried.

He popped the zoo hat on his head, waved to the brown animal with the big tongue, and waddled off. Soon he marched under the turnstile and into the zoo.

Charlie looked around. Where should he go first?

Right there, in the first enclosure, was an unbelievably big, truly colossal animal. He was just walking into the water as Charlie arrived. Soon he was almost completely submerged.

Suddenly he opened up his great big mouth, showing a pair of huge teeth.

Do you know what this animal is? It is soft, brown, and has two cute little ears. What could it be? Charlie is showing you how it opens its mouth.

It is a hippopotamus! Hippopotami are vegetarians, which means they only eat plants, like grass. They spend most of the day in water, and come back onto land in the evenings. Their name—hippopotamus—means "river horse" in Greek, and that is where they are most comfortable—in the river. They look particularly impressive when they yawn, with their huge mouths gaping wide open.

Unfortunately hippos are still being hunted, particularly for their beautifully curved canine teeth, or tusks, which are made of precious ivory.

In parts of Africa they are already extinct. Today, hippos are only found south of the Sahara desert. Hippos in the wild live to be about forty years old; in zoos they can live up to fifty.

Next door to the hippos, Charlie saw some really funny-looking animals. They had orange-brown fur, and arms that were longer than their legs. They swung around on vines and branches. They were real acrobats! Charlie wished he could do that too!

Do you know what these animals are? Their name means "forest person" in Malaysian.

They're orangutans! Orangutans live in the rainforests of Borneo and northern Sumatra. Unlike chimpanzees and gorillas, orangutans like to be alone.

These apes chiefly live in trees. They sleep high up in the branches, and every evening they build themselves a nest from branches and leaves. They love to eat fruit, but they also eat nuts, plants, bark, ants, and termites.

In the zoo they can live for fifty years. Orangutans are often hunted, and they are also threatened because the trees in the rainforests where they live are being cut down to be used as lumber, or to make room for crops.

Next Charlie stood for a long time in front of a big glass case, wondering what was inside. Finally, he noticed a green lizard. It crouched on a branch among the green leaves, and was nearly invisible.

When it moved, it crept very, very slowly. It looked like a tiny little dragon.

Do you know what this animal is? Its name comes from Greek, and means "earth-lion."

It's a chameleon! Half of all known chameleons live on
adagascar, an African island. They also live in other areas
Africa, Asia, and southern Spain.

The chameleon is a tree animal. It uses its long tail to
lance and climb. It can grab onto branches using its tail
a fifth leg. Chameleons' eyes can move independently,
they can look both forward and backward, or to the right
d left, at the same time.

As soon as a chameleon spots an insect, it flicks out its
gue to snap it up. The tip of the chameleon's tongue is like
suction cup, and its tongue is often longer than its body!

Chameleons can change their skin color to match their
surroundings, the temperature, or their mood. If
a chameleon is annoyed, for example, it will turn
very dark.

Charlie heard loud barking sounds coming from the other side of a big cliff. It was feeding time, and a zookeeper was there with the animals, getting them to perform tricks. Every time they did a trick, he rewarded them with a fish.

You might have seen these trained animals before. Do you know what they are?

They are sea lions! Sea lions eat squiggly squid, and lots of fish. They live up to twenty years.

The funny thing is, they don't just perform tricks in zoos. Even in the wild, they love to play around. Zookeepers just work with them to develop their natural talents.

Most of the sea lions that we see in zoos are California sea lions. Their bodies and heads are sleeker and narrower than other types of sea lions, which makes them look very graceful.

Sea lions move quite well on land, and have an outstanding sense of balance.

It was getting late. It was almost time to go home. Charlie's mother would be worrying about him. But there was one more thing Charlie just had to see.

At the zoo entrance, he'd seen a sign that showed where the baby animals were.

There they were—two small balls of fur trying to follow their mother, who lay high up in a tree, lazily swinging her long legs.

Do you know what animals have spotted fur and peek out from between the branches?

Leopards! Leopards have irregular spots, which are called rosettes. The rosettes are like flowers, where the petals are black and the center is tawny colored. Leopard means "lion-panther," because people once thought they were a mix of the two animals.

Leopards are loners. They like to find a spot high in a tree where they can easily see out into the distance. They hunt at night, and bring their catch back to the tree where they can eat it without being disturbed.

Leopards are found in parts of Africa, much of Asia, and into the far eastern reaches of Russia. In the wild, they can live as long as fifteen years. In zoos they can live up to twenty-five years.

When Charlie got home, he just had to tell everyone about what he had seen. He told them about the giant with the curved teeth, the swingy-armed acrobatic baby, the little dragon that didn't move, the fish-eater who swam and did tricks, and the spotted animal who balanced on the branch of a tree.

"Weren't you afraid?" asked the other ducklings, amazed.

"Afraid? No," Charlie said, shaking his head. "Well . . . there was one animal that did scare me. But it wasn't in the zoo—it lives right out there by our pond, in the *wild!* It has brown fur, and a huge, rough, wet tongue! I thought it was going to eat me!"

Do you know which animal Charlie meant?

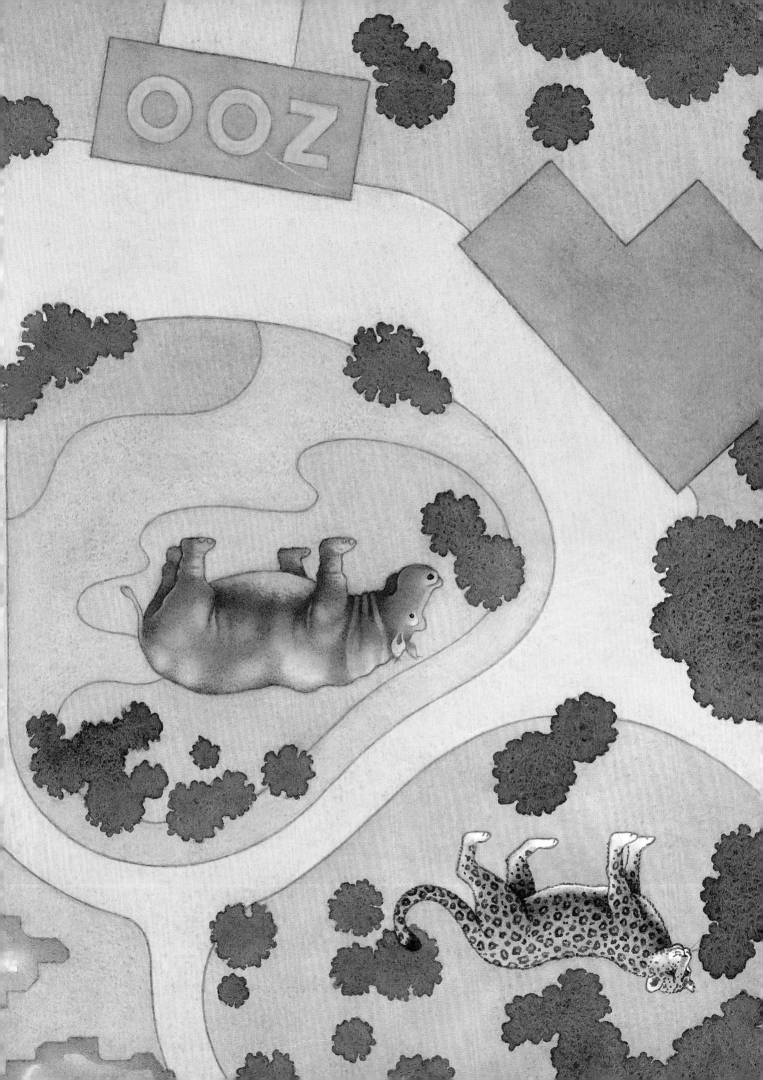